Mr. Putter & Tabby
Paint the Porch

CYNTHIA RYLANT

Mr. Putter & Tabby
Paint the Porch

Illustrated by

ARTHUR HOWARD

Harcourt, Inc.
San Diego   New York   London

For Bill and Susan's new little painter
—C. R.

To Cora Howard, who really knows how to paint a porch
—A. H.

Text copyright © 2000 by Cynthia Rylant
Illustrations copyright © 2000 by Arthur Howard

Library of Congress Cataloging-in-Publication Data
Rylant, Cynthia.
Mr. Putter & Tabby paint the porch/Cynthia Rylant;
illustrated by Arthur Howard.
p. cm.
Summary: Mr. Putter finds it a challenge to paint his front porch
in the presence of his cat, Tabby, and his neighbor's dog, Zeke.
[1. Cats—Fiction. 2. Dogs—Fiction. 3. Paint—Fiction.]
I. Howard, Arthur, ill. II. Title. III. Title: Mr. Putter and Tabby paint the porch.
PZ7.R982Msh 2000
[E]—dc21 98-51843
ISBN 0-15-201787-9

Printed in Singapore

First edition
A C E F D B

1

The Porch

It was springtime and Mr. Putter
and his fine cat, Tabby, were
feeling very chipper.
The birds sang, the sun shone,
the flowers bloomed.

Mr. Putter and Tabby went out
on the front porch with
a book.
"Let me read you a funny story,"
Mr. Putter said to Tabby.
Tabby purred.
She liked funny stories.

She curled up beside Mr. Putter
and waited.
And waited.
And waited.

But Mr. Putter was not looking
at the book.
He was looking at a porch post.
"Hmmm," said Mr. Putter.

He picked up Tabby and
looked more closely.
"Hmmm," he said again.
Mr. Putter walked all around the
porch, looking and saying, "Hmmm."

Finally he said, "Tabby, this
porch needs some paint.
First I am going to paint the porch.
Then I will read you a story."
Tabby purred.
She loved Mr. Putter's plans.
Especially when they included her.

She followed him to the basement,
swishing her tail,
happy it was spring.

2

Scat!

Mr. Putter carried his painting
things to the porch.
He had a bucket of pink paint,
a big brush,
and some rags.

Suddenly one of the rags got away.
Tabby chased it across the porch
and caught it.
"Good cat," said Mr. Putter,
patting her on the head.

Tabby purred.
She might be old, but she could
still catch a wild rag when
she had to.

Mr. Putter dipped his brush
into the bucket and began
to paint.

As he painted, he began to sing.
He sang about paper roses and
bluebonnets and
coming around mountains.

Tabby purred and purred.
This was even better than a story.
Mr. Putter didn't yodel
when he read a story.

All was going well when
suddenly a squirrel showed up.
The squirrel jumped onto a
freshly painted porch rail.
"Shoo!" said Mr. Putter.

The squirrel jumped onto
another rail.
"Scat!" said Mr. Putter.
Then the squirrel ran across
the floor of the porch.
"Scram!" said Mr. Putter.

And that's when Tabby remembered
how good she was at chasing things.
"Yikes!" yelled Mr. Putter.

The squirrel ran and Tabby ran.
And before it was all over,
Mr. Putter's porch just sort of
painted itself.

3

Very Pink

The next day Mr. Putter's porch
was very pink.
The walls were pink,
the floor was pink,
and even a few of the windows
were pink.

And Tabby was *very* pink.

Mr. Putter's neighbor
Mrs. Teaberry walked over
with her good dog, Zeke.
"Oh dear," she said, looking
at Mr. Putter's porch.
Zeke was sniffing Tabby's
pink whiskers.

Mr. Putter sighed.

"I have to do it all over again,"
he said.

"Well then, we will help," said
Mrs. Teaberry, rolling up her sleeves.

So Mr. Putter went back to
the basement.
Tabby followed, swishing her
pink tail.

Soon Mr. Putter and Mrs. Teaberry
were putting blue paint over pink.

And all was going well

until suddenly a chipmunk showed up.

It jumped on a rail.

It ran across the porch.

And then *Zeke* remembered how good *he* was at chasing chipmunks!

4

A Lovely Yellow

The next day Tabby and Zeke stayed
inside Mrs. Teaberry's house while
Mr. Putter painted his porch.
Again.
He covered up all of the pink
paw prints and all of the blue
paw prints and made the porch
a lovely yellow.

When the porch was dry,
Mrs. Teaberry arrived with Tabby
and Zeke.

Mr. Putter was happy to have
Tabby back.

He brought a book out on the porch
and said that he would read a
funny story to everyone.

But just as Mr. Putter was about
to begin, a pink squirrel and a blue
chipmunk walked by.

And Mr. Putter and Mrs. Teaberry
laughed so hard, they didn't
even *need* a funny story!

The illustrations in this book were done in pencil, watercolor,
gouache, and Sennelier pastels on 90-pound vellum paper.
The display type was set in Artcraft.
The text type was set in Berkeley Old Style Book.
Color separations by Tien Wah Press Limited, Singapore
Printed and bound by Tien Wah Press, Singapore
This book was printed on totally chlorine-free
Nymolla Matte Art paper.
Production supervision by Stanley Redfern
Designed by Arthur Howard and Carolyn Stafford